HOW TO
RAISE A LION

ISBN: 979-8-6666-6908-2

HOW TO
RAISE A LION

Written By
Ali Ellaboudy and Shereen Ulla

Illustrated by
Sadia Akter

I dedicate this book to Mustu, and Mama, and Baba, and my kitty cat, and me! Whoever wants to have a dedication, I can give them it.

Thank you to the lady who drew the pictures. Thank you to Mama and me because we made the book.

Thank you to Nanajaan for telling me about your tiger stories. Thank you to Nanima for telling me all of your funny and so crazy stories.

-Ali Ellaboudy

So many big thank you's for this little book. So much to explain about the how and the why of it all coming together. I must leave you with the words of A.A. Milne.

"My book is ready, and comes to greet
The mother it longs to see --
It would be my present to you, my sweet,
If it weren't your gift to me."

The House at Pooh Corner

-With my love, Shereen Ulla.

Bobo was a wild lion
everywhere he went.

His mama tried to tame him
every day she spent.

How to make him calm and mild?
Mama screamed and cried!

But Bobo didn't mind at all.
No matter how she tried.

Poor Mama couldn't keep up,
to a leash she had him attached.

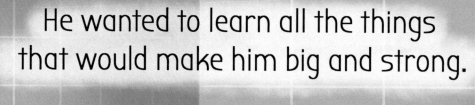

He wanted to learn all the things
that would make him big and strong.

Mama wanted to teach him all the ways
to know right from wrong.

So to the masjid, they both went to fix this little boy.
"Imam, how can I make him obedient but not overly coy?"

Then a big bearded laugh shook the Imam's belly,
at her request for something made with
peanut butter and jelly.

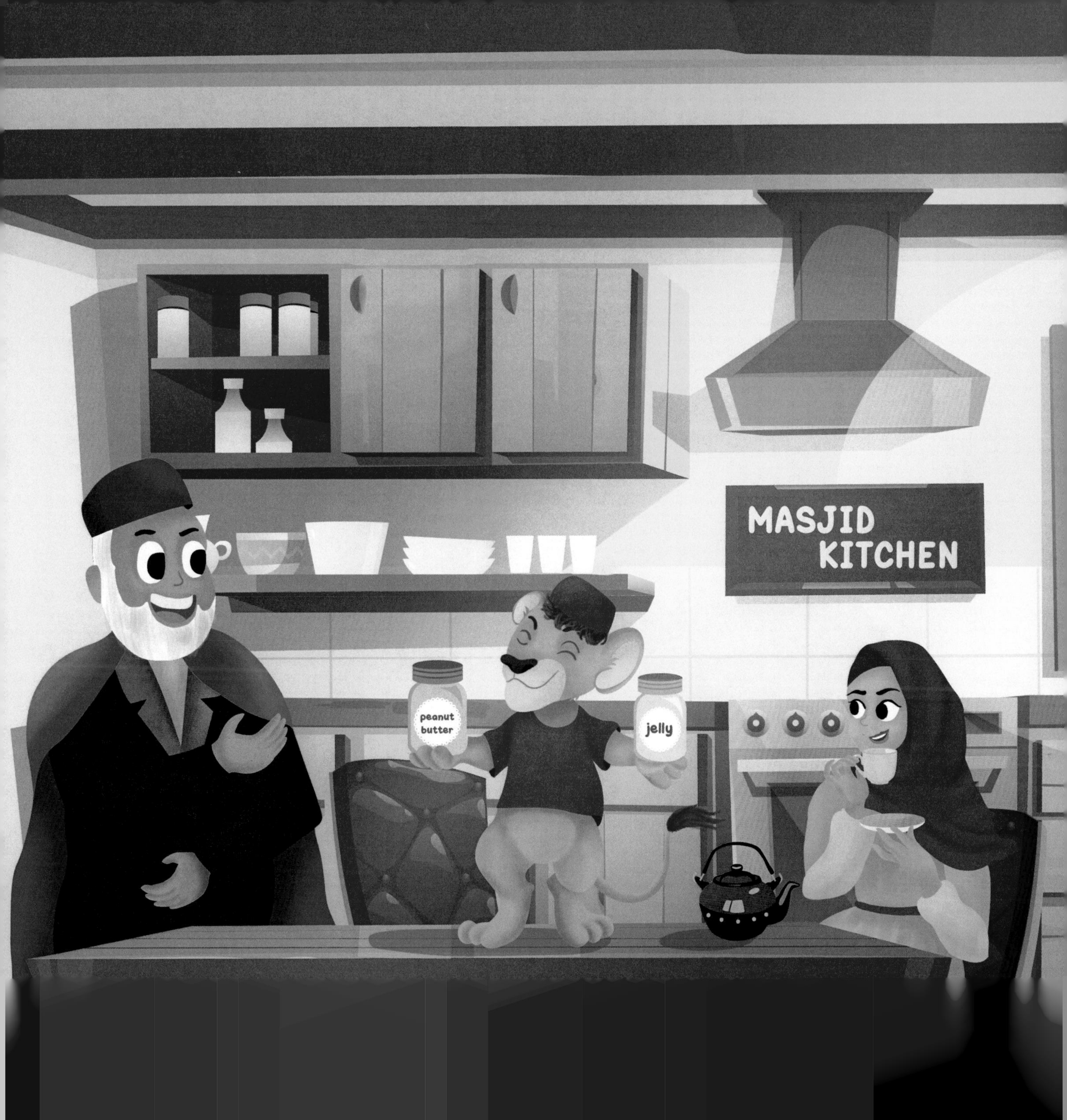
MASJID
KITCHEN
peanut
butter
jelly

He is a child, not a sandwich!
You can't assemble him to your taste.

You can try, as I've seen before,
but your efforts will all go to waste.

"He is joyful and carefree, so just let him play. Perhaps one day he may lead us all."

"As for now, let him be.
For childhood is a guest that will never stay."

GLOSSARY

Imam

Origin: Arabic

Synonym for leader. One who leads prayer in the Islamic faith.
Head of the community for Muslims.

Masjid

Origin: Arabic

Synonym for mosque. Place of worship for Muslims.

Made in United States
North Haven, CT
30 June 2023